GOOD IDEAS...

and Other Disasters

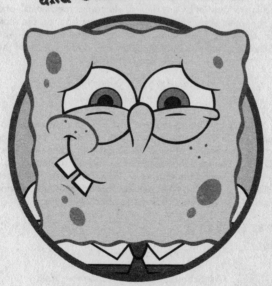

by Rebecca McCarthy

SCHOLASTIC INC.
New York Toronto London Auckland Sydney
Mexico City New Delhi Hong Kong Buenos Aires

Stephen Hillenburg

Based on the TV Series *SpongeBob SquarePants*® created by Stephen Hillenburg as seen on Nickelodeon®

ISBN-13: 978-0-545-07723-1
ISBN-10: 0-545-07723-0

12 11 10 9 8 7 6 5 4 3 2 1   8 9 10 11 12 13/0

Printed in the U.S.A.

First Scholastic printing, September 2008

THE OCEANIC TIMES 🐚

Good is bursting out all over!

The town of Bikini Bottom has been hit by an epidemic of epic proportions, and this latest sensation does not seem to be a passing trend. What is going on, you might ask? Well, Bikini Bottom has been hit by a whirlwind of good deeds!

What spurred all this goodwill toward others? Apparently it all started with a Bikini Bottom fry cook named SpongeBob SquarePants . . .

Table of Contents

Can you believe all the good stuff that's been happening in Bikini Bottom? Good is bursting out everywhere! There's just no stopping all the good deeds that people are trying to do.

Although the good deeds have also caused a crash, and an emergency visit to the hospital, everything turned out great in the end . . . really. You see, when you do something good for someone, good things happen to you in return, except when something bad happens to you in return, but even then that bad thing can turn into a good thing, uh, eventually . . . so everything that was bad ends up being good. Get it? Good!

It Takes Two to Tango

Okay, it all started one beautiful morning in Bikini Bottom. I was standing outside the Krusty Krab, and thinking about Mrs. Puff, who was recovering from my last driving lesson. I wished there was some way I could thank her for trying so hard to help me get my license.

Just then someone handed me a flyer. It said, "Bikini Bottom's Fifth Annual Square Dance. Lads, bring your ladies down to the chilly N. C. Bass Dance Hall for a rootin' tootin' good time!"

That's it! I thought. I'll take Mrs. Puff to the square dance!

When Mrs. Puff and I arrived, we took our places on the dance floor. The caller began to sing, but it was a lot faster and harder than I thought it would be!

Walk around the coral, partner do-si-do,
Partner by the ol' left fin, seashell right, you know,
Promenade left, sea star right, straight across
   the sea,
To a tailfin whirl, find the corner girl, now bait
   the hook for me.

Quick! I thought. Gotta keep up with the music!
I grabbed Mrs. Puff's right fin, swung her around the
floor, then tried a do-si-do, but I ended up bumping into
the guy in front of me. Then we tailfin-whirled into the
fiddle player, promenaded into the punch bowl, crashed
through the wall, and landed in the parking lot!

A police officer came over and said, "SpongeBob

SquarePants, I do hereby revoke your dancing privileges. Citizens of Bikini Bottom, remember: You must be able to keep your feet on the floor to dance . . . squarely!"

I really wanted to do something nice for Mrs. Puff, and I ended up getting her into another crash—and losing my dancing privileges! This good idea turned out all wrong!

A Seaweed Pie a Day . . .

Oh, SpongeBob is quite the nondriver, but little did I know that he was an even worse square dancer! But you know something? I really appreciated the fact that he wanted to do something nice for me. So the next day I felt inspired to do something nice for someone else.

I decided to bake one of my famous seaweed pies and bring it over to Mr. Krabs for a picnic lunch. I baked all morning, put the pie in a basket, tied a ribbon around it, and strolled down to the Krusty Krab. Mr. Krabs was very happy to see me, and we went outside to sit in a nice, shady picnic area. He happily scooped up a large forkful of pie and said, "Mmm . . . that's delicious! What is it?"

"It's my famous seaweed pie!" I answered.

Mr. Krabs's face froze. "Did you say, 'seaweed pie'?"

Suddenly he started to gasp and wheeze. Through coughs and gags I could make out the words, "Allergic. Seaweed. Hospital." Oh, no! Mr. Krabs is allergic to seaweed!

Mr. Krabs started puffing up under his shell. He looked like a parade balloon! We rushed him to the hospital, and it took a few hours before he was finally back to normal.

And then the doctor came in with the bill, which made Mr. Krabs feel a whole lot worse. "What!" he exclaimed. "Are ye crazy?"

"Well, I can just put this seaweed back into your stomach and—," said the doctor.

"No, no! I'll pay it," said Mr. Krabs, anxious to avoid another run-in with seaweed.

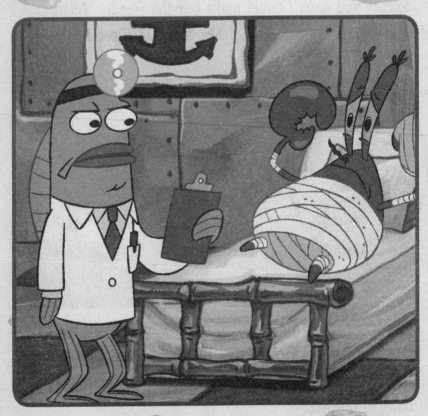

After he paid the bill I apologized, gathered my things, and went home. My good deed didn't do Mr. Krabs much good at all!

Money Isn't Everything . . . Is It?

It was awfully kind of Mrs. Puff to bring me a picnic lunch. Even though it didn't have the happiest ending, it's the thought that counts. So I thought I would try to do somethin' nice for someone else.

I got the chance when me daughter Pearl came running into the restaurant, sobbin'. Seems there was a fin-hop at her school gym that night, but she couldn't go because she had already offered to babysit for the Poecilia family up the road. "Life is cruel!" she cried. "I want to go to the dance!" Then she blew her nose into one of me hankies.

Suddenly the idea struck me like a ton o'money: I should take over the babysittin' shift for Pearl so that she can go to the fin-hop! It would be nice for her, and it meant extra money for me. Now that's what I call win-win!

Little did I know, the Poecilias have *twenty-six* young 'uns, and they're all menaces! Jimmy spilled some finger paint on the rug. I found Petey in the kitchen eatin' a whole box of Fun Flakes. Cindy told me her tummy hurt because she swallowed a crayon. Then Benny, Jenny, Kenny, and Lenny started screamin' and cryin' in the playroom while Jill and Bill threw toys out the window. Barnacles! This job turned out to be a lot more than I bargained for!

At bedtime I told the kiddies a story from me
old sailin' days. But once I mentioned Davy Jones and
his ghost pirate ship, the children got scared. And
when their mum and dad came home, all twenty-six
scallywags were sobbin' and hollerin'.

"What is going on here, Mr. Krabs?" Mrs. Poecilia asked. She was angry!

"Well, I tried to tell them an exciting bedtime story, but I guess it scared them too much," I explained.

"Well, then, I guess we'll just have to send you home with *no pay!*" she said.

"No pay?" I gasped. Then *I* started cryin' and kept it goin' all the way home!

The Early Bird Catches the Worm

It sure was nice of Daddy to babysit for me. I had a totally tubular time at the fin-hop! In fact that night I passed by Squidward's house and thought, I should do something nice for Squidward since my daddy did something nice for me.

So the next morning I got up early and went to the city pound. I picked out the sweetest little wormy I could find, and brought it over to Squidward's. When he answered the door I said, "Good morning, Uncle Squiddy! I'm doing a good deed today and here it is!" I handed the leash over to him, and then headed for the mall.

After shopping, I stopped by Squidward's again to see how he was getting along with his new pet.

Squidward was not happy. "Well, after you left," he said, "I went to the pet store and bought a bag of worm food, and the worm ate the whole thing right up! And when I went to make myself some lunch, he ate up all the ingredients! In five minutes this adorable, cutesy-wootsy little worm had eaten all the food in my kitchen! Pearl, you are going to have to take this beast back home with you!"

"Oh, no! My good deed went majorly wrong!" I said. "I'm sorry, Squidward."

As I turned to pick up the worm, Squidward said, "I've got to relax. This worm has stressed me out."

So he picked up his clarinet and started playing. And wouldn't you know it, something totally beachy happened. The worm sat up and wagged his tail. And when Squidward finished playing, he applauded by thumping his tail on the floor. There was no doubt that this worm loved Squidward's clarinet playing!

Suddenly Squidward changed his mind. "I'm going to keep him!" he announced. "This worm is terrific, Pearl. I think I'll name him Mishka!"

"Goody!" I said, jumping up and clapping my hands. "Okay, I gotta go!"

Before Squidward could start playing his clarinet again, I headed for the door. "See you later!"

Every Squid Has His Day

It was nice of Pearl to bring me Mishka. I played the clarinet all night long and he loved it. I decided to share my good fortune with others, and that was when I saw Sandy with a hammer and nails, putting up a poster at the Krusty Krab.

"Hi, there, Squidward!" she said, "I'm having an art auction tomorrow to raise money for scientific research."

Well, that's right up my alley, I thought. I'll paint a portrait and donate it to Sandy's auction. Sometimes I amaze myself with my brilliant ideas.

On the day of the auction I brought my masterpiece, *Squidward: Perfection in Paint*, to City Hall. I set it on an easel between a velvet Elvis and a painting of some poker players.

When it came time to bid on the painting, the auctioneer said, "Well, folks, this next item is a picture of, uh, well, it's a picture. Let's start the bidding at, uh . . . do I hear, five cents?" The room was silent.

I dashed out of the room and came back disguised as a famous art collector. I stood up and said, "That piece of artwork is both thrilling and riveting. Whoever painted this is a genius! I think the bidding should start at one hundred dollars!"

The auctioneer called out, "One hundred dollars from the gentleman with the funny hat. Do I hear one twenty?" Again there was silence. I slipped out of the room and came back disguised as a wealthy lady. "I bid one fifty!" I shouted.

"One fifty from the lady with the feather boa," said the auctioneer, "Do I hear two hundred?" Nobody made another bid. Then suddenly the auctioneer said, "Going once, going twice, sold to the lady with the feather boa for one hundred and fifty dollars!"

I could not believe it! I had to spend all my savings to buy back my own art! Some good deed this turned out to be. Now I'm broke!

The Sun Will Come Out Tomorrow

Thanks to Squidward's donation to my auction, I was able to buy parts to build a new rocket ship! Patrick came over and asked if he could ride in it with me.

"Well, you're not really trained to be an astronaut," I told Patrick, "but you know what? I'm going to teach you everything you need to know. Welcome aboard!"

"Oh, boy! Oh, boy!" Patrick said. "We're going on a rocket ship to . . . uh, where are we going?"

"We're going to explore the sun!" I said. "I've built these special heat shields so the ship won't burn up. Even though it'll be hotter than a griddle outside, we'll be cooler than frozen cow juice inside."

I named Patrick my first commanding officer, and we climbed inside the ship. "Now, this is the control panel," I explained. "The green buttons are used for liftoff. And over here is a keypad with numbers on it. You just punch in the landing code to bring the ship down. And over here—"

Before I could continue, Patrick leaned over and asked, "What does this button do?"—and pressed it. Suddenly an alarm sounded.

"No, that's the self-destruct button!" I cried. Patrick panicked and started punching numbers and pulling levers, and things started going crazy. We had no choice but to abandon ship!

The rocket fell apart, and the heat shields were beyond repair.

"I'm sorry, Sandy," said Patrick.

"Oh, that's all right, Patrick," I said. "I can rebuild this ship in two shakes of a lamb's tail. I don't have any money left to buy new heat shields, though, so we won't be able to take that trip to the sun after all. Not unless you've got any bright ideas about how to get us up there without burnin' up."

"Well," Patrick said thoughtfully, "what if we just go at night?"

That Patrick may have destroyed my rocket ship, but he makes me laugh harder than a pack of hyenas!

He Who Awaits Much Receives Little

Sandy was supernice to let me come over and play inside the rocket ship. It made me feel warm and happy. So I decided to make someone else feel warm and happy. When I passed by a building with a sign out front that said ALGAE ON WHEELS: VOLUNTEERS NEEDED, I went inside to volunteer.

The guy at the front desk explained that volunteers deliver food to elderly citizens who don't have boats. He gave me a bag full of groceries, and told me to take it to Old Man Jenkins, who lives at the edge of Bikini Bottom.

I rode the bus all the way out to Old Man Jenkins's house. While on the bus I got hungry and ate up all the food that was supposed to be for him. When I got to his house I told Old Man Jenkins that I would be right back with a new bag of food.

The second time I rode my skateboard and wiped out! All the food ended up on the ground.

All this volunteering made me tired, so I asked Old Man Jenkins if I could come inside and take a nap.

When I woke up, Old Man Jenkins was standing over me saying, "I've had enough of waitin', boy. I'm starvin'!" Then he grabbed his cane, hobbled all the way to the Algae on Wheels headquarters, picked up a bag of food, and hobbled home.

"Glad I could help out today!" I said, when I left his house. Good deeds are nice.

A Plankton Never Changes His Spots

That young whippersnapper sure left me hungry, but it was nice that he wanted to help. I decided to see if I could help someone else.

On the road I almost stepped on a wee little fella. He said his name was Plankton and that he needed to get the recipe for Krabby Patties. "Well, I'll help you," I said. "Where's this recipe?"

"It's in a safe in the back room of the Krusty Krab," said Plankton.

I walked through the front door of the Krusty Krab, toward the rear of the restaurant where someone sat reading *Dancers Weekly* magazine. I walked past him and into the back room, where a yellow fella flipped patties on a grill.

I walked past him to a vault, turned the combination lock a few times, opened the door, and found the "secret Krabby Patty recipe" in a bottle. I took the recipe out of the bottle, read it, placed it back in the vault, closed the door, walked past the patty flipper, the magazine reader, and out the door. "Thanks, come again," said the guy. He didn't even look up from his magazine.

Outside, Plankton asked, "Well, what's the recipe?"

I opened my mouth to speak, and then looked blankly at him.

"I forget," I finally said, then shuffled back to my house. It was time for my medication, and my legs were starting to hurt. I'm not as young as I used to be, you know.

As I passed by a tree I heard a "Meow." I looked up and saw a snail stuck on a limb. I raised my cane and let the little creature crawl onto it, and then I lowered him gently to the ground. "Well, how do you like that?" I realized. "I just did a good deed!"

It just goes to show, you're never too old to help out a fellow citizen.

Big Things Come in Small Shells

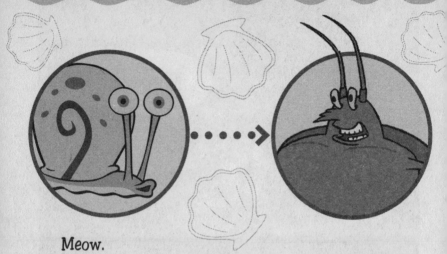

Meow.

Translation: After Old Man Jenkins helped me down from the tree, I passed by Mussel Beach on my way home. I saw Larry the Lobster having an argument with a bodybuilder named Gustavus.

"My muscles are bigger than yours," Gustavus boasted. "I can surf better, and I have bigger biceps. I am also a better lifeguard than you!" A crowd began to form.

"Dude, your muscles may be bigger, but my, um . . . I'm . . . better at, uh . . .," Larry stammered. He couldn't think of a smart comeback, and everyone laughed.

I went up to Larry and nudged his leg. "Meow," I said. And Larry understood.

"Hey, Gustavus," he called out, "How'd you like to compete in a clam press contest? You see that trough full of clams over there? It weighs one hundred pounds, and I bet I can lift it."

So Larry bent down, lifted the trough high over his head, then put it down. Gustavus laughed. "This is too easy," he said smugly.

While everyone was busy watching Gustavus prepare to lift the trough, I climbed up the side, slipping in to hide among the clams. Now the trough weighed one hundred pounds *and three ounces*.

Sure enough, Gustavus bent down to pick up the trough—but he couldn't do it! Larry won the contest!

"Three cheers for Bikini Bottom's strongest lifeguard! Hip, hip, hooray!" everyone cheered. Larry smiled at me. "Thanks, little dude. I owe you one."

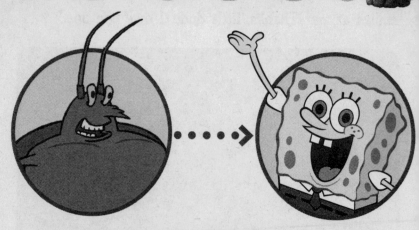

It was awesome when Gary helped me out today. I decided it would be fantastic if I could help someone else out too. I noticed SpongeBob sitting out on the dock, looking kinda down. "What's wrong, little fella?" I asked.

"Nothing," he said, then he wailed, "I'm just so upset over what happened at the square dance. I ruined everything!"

What usually helps me when I feel down is a beach party. So I said, "Let's have a beach party!"

Soon we had a bunch of his friends at the beach for a rockin' luau. And they all had nice things to say.

"Meow."
Translation: "I helped Larry win a clam press contest because Old Man Jenkins helped me down when I was stuck up a tree."

"I helped that little snail out of a tree because a nice young man tried to bring me my groceries."

"Uh, I tried to bring groceries, but I got hungry. . . . Hey, these pineapple thingies are good!"

"Patrick and I got to work on my rocket ship because Squidward made a generous donation to my art auction."

"Well, I donated to the art auction because Pearl gave me a new pet, Mishka."

"I got Squidward a pet because my daddy babysat for me so I could go to the fin-hop!"

"Well, I did that because sweet Mrs. Puff made me a seaweed pie."

"And I made Mr. Krabs that pie because SpongeBob was so kind to take me to the square dance. Even though it didn't turn out very well, it was the thought that counted, and the thought was very, very good."

"Well, look at that. My good deed wasn't a disaster after all. And everyone started helping everyone else out!"

It's like I said in the beginning, when your heart is in the right place, everything turns out for the best. Even when things look bad, they can be good. Even when things look disastrous, they can be good. Even when things look hopeless and horrible . . . they can be *good*!

Hey, who wants me to house-sit while they're on vacation? Who needs me to take them to the hospital? Who wants me to teach road-safety classes? Who wants me to help them carry something? Anyone? Don't all speak up at once! Uh . . . hello?